1, 3, 5, 8,

Associated Board Brass Scales and Arpeggios

Series Editors **John Wallace** and **Ian Denley**

Scales and Arpeggios for Trombone, Bass Trombone, Baritone and Euphonium 𝄢

Grades 1-8

It is often maintained, with some justification, that brass-players frequently show reluctance to learn scales and arpeggios thoroughly. But as they form the basis of a fluent technique and help to stabilize range and accuracy, a methodical and thorough preparation of scales and arpeggios is essential.

This manual seeks to assist this situation by including comprehensive fingering and trombone slide position charts, together with hints on problems to avoid and useful advice appended to the scales and arpeggios most likely to be problematic. The aim is to help students learn their scales and arpeggios thoroughly, as well as provide support material for those brass teachers who may not be specialists on this group of instruments.

Given the wide range of instruments catered for in this manual, we are most grateful to the following team of contributing specialist advisers: Dudley Bright, Principal Trombone with the Philharmonia Orchestra and Professor at the Royal Academy of Music; Peter Walker, a member of the brass teaching team of the North Yorkshire Education Authority; Bob Childs, Head of Brass at Hymers College, Hull, and Principal Euphonium of the Black Dyke Mills Brass Band; and Patrick Harrild, Principal Tuba with the London Symphony Orchestra and Professor at the Royal Academy of Music and the Guildhall School of Music.

JOHN WALLACE and IAN DENLEY 1995

The Associated Board of the Royal Schools of Music

Trombone slide position chart

This comprehensive slide position chart applies to the trombone when it is read in bass clef and to the bass trombone. It gives the standard slide positions, together with alternatives available from the 'F' thumb valve (known also as the 'plug' or 'trigger') and indicates slide length adjustments which may be necessary in the upper register (see p.6 for details of these measurements).

The first five notes (B–Eb) apply only to the bass trombone in the examination requirements. See note on the bass trombone on p.5 for important information on these notes.

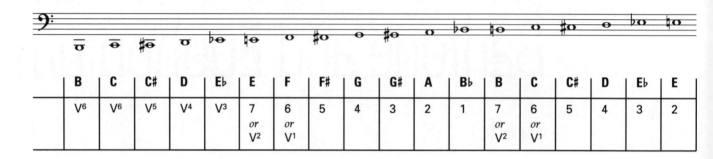

B	C	C#	D	Eb	E	F	F#	G	G#	A	Bb	B	C	C#	D	Eb	E
V⁶	V⁶	V⁵	V⁴	V³	7 or V²	6 or V¹	5	4	3	2	1	7 or V²	6 or V¹	5	4	3	2

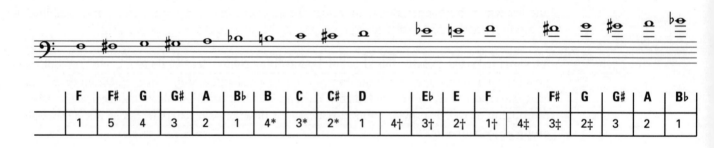

F	F#	G	G#	A	Bb	B	C	C#	D	Eb	E	F	F#	G	G#	A	Bb
1	5	4	3	2	1	4*	3*	2*	1	4†	3†	2†	1†	4‡	3‡	2‡	3	2	1

Key to symbols

1-7	basic slide positions	
V¹-V⁶	basic slide positions + 'F' thumb valve (see p.5)	

* ⎫
† ⎬ These symbols indicate the various slide adjustments necessary to improve tuning. See note on intonation on p.6.
‡ ⎭

Valved instrument fingering chart

This comprehensive fingering chart applies to the baritone and euphonium which read in the bass clef. Both standard and alternative fingerings available to these instruments are given. Additional information is given in the annotations attached to the scales and arpeggios.

The first six fingerings (B♭–E♭), which are for notes below the range required in the Associated Board's examinations, are included for their presence in some repertoire. The shaded fingerings are available only to euphoniums which have a 4th valve (see note on the 4th valve on p.7).

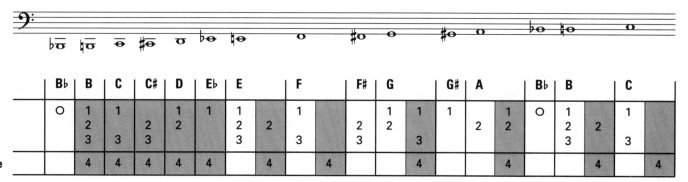

	B♭	B	C	C♯	D	E♭	E	F	F♯	G	G♯	A	B♭	B	C
Fingering	O	1 2 3	1 3	2 3	1 2	1	1 2 3 / 2	1 3	2 3	1 2	1	2	O	1 2 3 / 2	1 3
4th valve		4	4	4	4	4	4	4		4		4		4	4

	C♯	D	E♭	E	F	F♯	G	G♯	A	B♭	B	C	C♯
Fingering	2 3	1 2 / 3	1 / 3	2 / 1 2 3	O / 1 3	1 2 3	1 2 / 3	1 / 1 2 3	2 / 1 3	1 / O / 2 3	1 2 / 3	1 / 1 3	2 / 2 3

	D	E♭	E	F	F♯	G	G♯	A	B♭
Fingering	O / 1 2	1 / 1 3	1 / 2 / 1 2 3	O / 1 / 1 3	2 3	1 / 1 2 / 2	3 / 1 / 1 2 3	O / 1 / 2 / 1 2	1 3 / 1 / O / 2 3	1
4th valve			4		4	4			

Key to symbols

1 press index finger	3 press ring finger	4 press 4th valve (euphonium only).
2 press middle finger	O all fingers off	Usually played by the LH middle finger.

Table of harmonics

As a source for the exploration of alternative fingerings, the following table illustrates the notes available from each combination of valves (i.e. each length of tubing). This is known as the *harmonic series*. The first note in each row is the 'fundamental' or 'pedal note'. The numbered notes which follow the fundamental, obtainable from each valve combination by embouchure adjustment, are known as *harmonics*, or *upper partials*.

The fundamental note is only occasionally used. Strictly speaking, there is no upper limit to the harmonic series, but it must be stressed that these extremes of range should only be undertaken by the highly advanced player. As they feature in some of the more complex repertoire they are included here for reference.

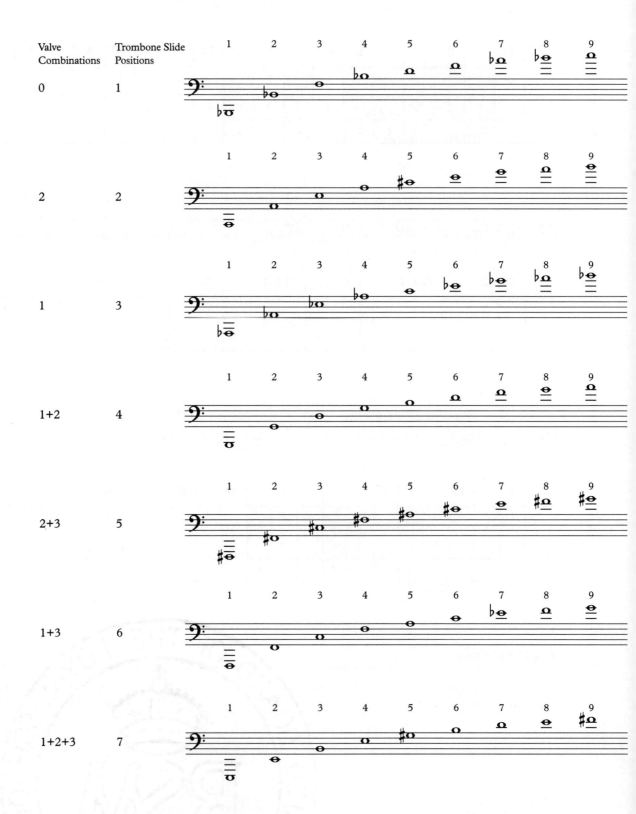

Guide to trombone slide positions

For reference purposes, where notes are indicated throughout the manual with a small superscript number (e.g. Bb^1, E^2, $F\sharp^3$, etc.), this refers to their position within the trombone's range:

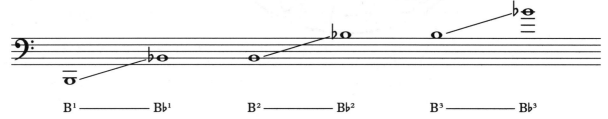

The range of notes within the Associated Board's scales and arpeggios is from E^1 to Bb^3 (B^1 to G^3 for the bass trombone).

Slide positions

There are very few alternative positions which are used in scales and arpeggios. Those given for some notes in the upper register may be tried, but should be discarded if found to be unsatisfactory.

In reality, it is virtually impossible to measure the slide positions accurately, but it is important to be aware of their relative location and to understand that each position extends slightly further than the last. This will help avoid the common occurrence among inexperienced players of playing progressively sharper as the slide is extended further.

The following diagram illustrates the approximate measurement in centimetres of each slide position, as measured from the 1st or closed position:

position	1	2	3	4	5	6	7
cm.	0	8	16.5	26.5	37	48	60

'F' valve alternatives

Where available, the 'F' valve is used to avoid the long stretch of the 6th and 7th positions:

'F' valve + 1st position (V^1) = 6th position   'F' valve + 2nd position (V^2) = 7th position

NB: when using the 'F' valve with 2nd position (V^2), the slide should be extended to a length of 10 cm., not 8.

The bass trombone

The bass trombone has an extended lower range achieved by using the 'F' valve in conjunction with positions 3 to 6. It should be noted that to do this it is necessary to extend the slide further than normal for positions 3 to 6, so that eventually 6th position occupies what is normal placing for 7th position.

The Associated Board's requirements for bass trombone take the instrument down to low B (B^1), a note not obtainable on the single-valve bass trombone by ordinary means. To obtain B^1 for the two requirements at Grade 8, the 'F' valve slide should be extended so that the note can be obtained in 6th position and all other positions adjusted accordingly, the student listening carefully to the tuning. The large variety of configuration of two-valve bass trombones means that the way B^1 is obtained on these instruments varies greatly and players should consult the manufacturer's specification.

Intonation

The trombonist must learn to master intonation in the seven standard positions through careful listening, both to himself (or herself) and others with whom he (she) might be playing.

Due to the nature of its slide mechanism, perfect intonation on the trombone is more immediately accessible than on valved brass instruments. Whilst not every note in each position is exactly in tune, the slide can be used to make slight adjustments.

The slide position chart indicates, with the symbols *, † and ‡, those notes which may require adjustments to improve the tuning. In the measurements below, *minus* quantities indicate that the slide should be drawn *towards* the player by the suggested amount; *plus* quantities indicate that the slide should be extended *away* from the player.

 * = –2-5mm. † = +5-10mm. ‡ = –15-20mm.

These are given only as a guide, as intonation varies between instruments. The importance of careful listening cannot be stressed enough in determining the extent of these small but significant adjustments.

Care should be taken to ensure that all notes are centred at their true pitch before slide adjustments are made. This skill is developed by a constant and discriminating attention to both tone quality and intonation.

Maintenance

It is important that the main slide and tuning slides be kept lubricated for optimum performance.

Enharmonic note-names

Two or three notes having the same sound but different names are called *enharmonics*; for example, E♭ is the enharmonic of D♯. A full table is given below to guide students in the fingering of those notes in certain scales and arpeggios which may be unfamiliarly notated.

C	=	B♯	=	D♭♭		E	=	F♭	=	D𝄪		G♯	=	A♭
C♯	=	D♭	=	B𝄪		F	=	E♯	=	G♭♭		A	=	G𝄪 = B♭♭
D	=	C𝄪	=	E♭♭		F♯	=	G♭	=	E𝄪		B♭	=	A♯ = C♭♭
E♭	=	D♯	=	F♭♭		G	=	F𝄪	=	A♭♭		B	=	C♭ = A𝄪

Guide to valved instruments

For reference purposes, where notes are indicated throughout the manual with a small superscript number (e.g. B♭[1], E[2], F♯[3], etc.), this refers to their position within the range of this family of brass instruments:

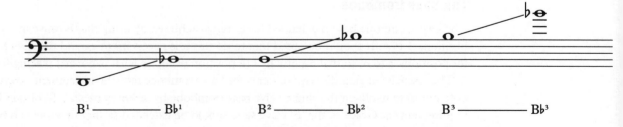

The range of notes within the Associated Board's scales and arpeggios is from E[1] to B♭[3].

Posture, fingering and grip

The importance of developing a good posture (frequently overlooked by brass players) is essential in the process of natural breathing, which is vital in the study of scales and arpeggios. The parts of the body involved must be kept comfortably in balance, whether standing or sitting.

For really fluent scales and arpeggios the hand depressing the valves must be relaxed. Most of the weight bearing of the instrument should be taken by the other hand. A sideways pressure when depressing a valve should be avoided as it will impair the valve action.

The 4th valve (euphonium only)

The 4th valve is the most common additional valve found on the euphonium. It provides an excellent opportunity for options in tuning, as well as facility in fingering, and if available should always be used.

Intonation

Intonation and the careful negotiation of intervals should feature greatly in the study of scales and arpeggios. They are affected by many factors: the size of the oral cavity, the position of the tongue and the quality of the sound (quality of sound profoundly affects pitch).

Generally, the best fingering to use is the one that is in tune. This is especially true at the top of the range where the harmonics are closer together.

In the lower range E^1, B^2 and C^2, fingered 1+2+3, 1+2+3, and 1+3 respectively, are usually sharp on valved instruments. Euphonium players can compensate by using the alternative fingerings involving the 4th valve where this is available.

At the top of the range E♭, E and F are also usually sharp. Euphonium players again should compensate by using the 4th valve where available.

Baritone players should adjust the intonation of these notes with the embouchure, listening carefully.

Maintenance

It is important that all valves and tuning slides be kept lubricated for optimum performance.

Enharmonic note-names

Two or three notes having the same sound but different names are called *enharmonics*; for example, E♭ is the enharmonic of D♯. A full table is given below to guide students in the fingering of those notes in certain scales and arpeggios which may be unfamiliarly notated.

C	=	B♯	=	D♭♭		E	=	F♭	=	D×		G♯	=	A♭			
C♯	=	D♭	=	B×		F	=	E♯	=	G♭♭		A	=	G×	=	B♭♭	
D	=	C×	=	E♭♭		F♯	=	G♭	=	E×		B♭	=	A♯	=	C♭♭	
E♭	=	D♯	=	F♭♭		G	=	F×	=	A♭♭		B	=	C♭	=	A×	

Notes on the requirements

Reference must always be made to the syllabus for the year in which the examination is to be taken, in case any changes have been made to the requirements.

In the examination all scales and arpeggios must be played from memory.

Candidates should aim to play their scales and arpeggios at a pace that allows accuracy, with a uniform tone across all registers and a rhythmic flow without undue accentuation, as well as with even tonguing and good intonation. Recommended speeds for all instruments are given on page 10.

In Grades 1-5 candidates may choose *either* the melodic *or* the harmonic form of the minor scale; in Grades 6-8 candidates are required to play *both* forms.

The choice of breathing place is left to the candidate's discretion, but taking a breath must not be allowed to disturb the flow of the scale or arpeggio. In the case of valved instruments, if a breath is taken during the course of a slurred scale or arpeggio, a soft tongue attack should be made on the note following the breath.

It is desirable that students do not use a breath as a means of disguising an embouchure 'break', where the position of the lips on the mouthpiece has to be re-seated as the player moves from one register to another in the course of a scale or arpeggio. Whilst embouchure breaks are quite common, it is preferable to be free from them as they do cause difficulties and can be avoided.

Articulation

It is very important for the foundation of good articulation that players use the *tongue* to articulate, rather than just the breath, which is a common error at the elementary level. The sound must be well-supported by diaphragmatic breathing throughout all forms of articulation, so that the tone does not deteriorate (usually with attendant intonation problems), especially when tonguing *staccato*.

Four different forms of articulation are found in the scale and arpeggio requirements: slurred, tongued, *legato*-tongued and *staccato*.

Valved instruments	In Grades 1-6 candidates are required to play scales and arpeggios both slurred and tongued; in Grades 7 and 8 candidates are required to play scales and arpeggios slurred, *legato*-tongued and *staccato*.
Trombone	In Grades 1-6 candidates are required to play scales and arpeggios both tongued and *legato*-tongued; in Grades 7 and 8 candidates are required to play scales and arpeggios tongued, *legato*-tongued and *staccato*.

In slurred scales and arpeggios there is no gap between the notes, whereas the gap is large when playing *staccato*. In *legato*-tonguing, the effect is almost slurred, but there is the smallest separation achieved by a very soft tongue attack.

The articulations may be visualized like this:

slurred

tongued

legato-tongued

staccato

Legato-tonguing is often considered by brass players to be a fusion of *tenuto* and *legato*; it is sometimes described as 'soft'-tonguing or as an articulated slur. Perhaps the least familiar of the articulation forms required, it may usefully be notated as follows:

Considerations for the trombonist

It is especially important that trombonists make a clear distinction between tongued and *legato*-tongued in all grades. Trombonists do not have the option of slurring in the accepted sense of the word and must develop a really smooth and accurate slide-control from the earliest stages to expect real success in achieving *legato* effects on their instrument. This is best achieved by moving the slide as quickly as possible, without gripping or jerking it. The major difficulty lies in avoiding smears or *glissando*s when the slide has to move in the same direction as the pitch.

A 'soft' consonant should be used to tongue as the slide is moved. It should be soft enough to keep the *legato* smooth without interrupting the sound, but firm enough to avoid making a *glissando*.

A relaxed posture and open throat will help keep the breath flow even and continuous, thereby avoiding bulges and unscheduled accents in what should be essentially smooth lines.

Current requirements for Grades 1-8

These tables list scales and arpeggios required for each grade; numbers refer to those printed alongside the scales and arpeggios in the following pages.

Trombone

Grade 1   24, 28 *or* 29, 126, 130

Grade 2   1, 19, 28 *or* 29, 38 *or* 39, 103, 121, 130, 135

Grade 3   7, 10, 20, 38 *or* 39, 62 *or* 63, 82, 109, 112, 122, 135, 147

Grade 4   4, 20, 25, 50 *or* 51, 62 *or* 63, 86, 106, 122, 127, 141, 147

Grade 5   14, 16, 18, 22, 30 *or* 31, 54 *or* 55, 64 *or* 65, 89, 116, 118, 120, 124, 131, 143, 148, 167

Grade 6   2, 13, 21, 25, 34, 35, 58, 59, 76, 77, 91, 93, 104, 115, 123, 129, 133, 145, 154, 157, 172

Grade 7   2, 5, 8, 11, 13, 14, 16, 18, 21, 23, 26, 27, 30, 31, 34, 35, 40, 41, 46, 47, 52, 53, 54, 55, 58, 59, 64, 65, 68, 69, 72, 73, 78, 79, 80, 81, 88, 89, 90, 91, 93, 94, 97, 104, 107, 110, 113, 115, 116, 118, 120, 123, 125, 128, 129, 131, 133, 136, 139, 142, 143, 145, 148, 150, 152, 155, 156, 158, 168, 174, 176

Grade 8   2, 5, 8, 11, 13, 14, 16, 18, 21, 23, 26, 27, 30, 31, 34, 35, 40, 41, 46, 47, 52, 53, 54, 55, 58, 59, 64, 65, 68, 69, 72, 73, 78, 79, 80, 81, 88, 89, 90, 91, 93, 94, 97, 99, 100, 104, 107, 110, 113, 115, 116, 118, 120, 123, 125, 128, 129, 131, 133, 136, 139, 142, 143, 145, 148, 150, 152, 155, 156, 157, 158, 159, 160, 166, 167, 168, 174, 175, 176

Bass Trombone

Grade 6   3, 9, 12, 20, 36, 37, 42, 43, 48, 49, 83, 84, 105, 111, 114, 122, 134, 137, 140, 166, 169

Grade 7   3, 6, 9, 12, 13, 14, 15, 17, 20, 22, 25, 27, 32, 33, 36, 37, 42, 43, 48, 49, 52, 53, 54, 55, 56, 57, 62, 63, 66, 67, 70, 71, 76, 77, 80, 81, 83, 84, 85, 87, 105, 108, 111, 114, 115, 116, 117, 119, 122, 124, 127, 129, 132, 134, 137, 140, 142, 143, 144, 147, 149, 151, 154, 156, 162, 164, 169, 170

Grade 8   3, 6, 9, 12, 13, 14, 16, 18, 20, 22, 25, 27, 32, 33, 36, 37, 42, 43, 48, 49, 52, 53, 54, 55, 58, 59, 64, 65, 66, 67, 70, 71, 76, 77, 80, 81, 83, 84, 85, 87, 98, 101, 102, 105, 108, 111, 114, 115, 116, 118, 120, 122, 124, 127, 129, 132, 134, 137, 140, 142, 143, 145, 148, 149, 151, 154, 156, 161, 162, 163, 164, 165, 169, 170, 171

Baritone and Euphonium

Grade 1 24, 60 *or* 61, 126, 146

Grade 2 1, 19, 28 *or* 29, 60 *or* 61, 103, 121, 130, 146

Grade 3 4, 7, 17, 38 *or* 39, 74 *or* 75, 95, 106, 109, 119, 135, 153

Grade 4 10, 15, 20, 44 *or* 45, 62 *or* 63, 70 *or* 71, 92, 112, 117, 122, 138, 147, 151

Grade 5 14, 16, 20, 27, 54 *or* 55, 66 *or* 67, 80 *or* 81, 96, 116, 118, 122, 129, 143, 149, 156, 167

Grade 6 2, 13, 18, 21, 58, 59, 64, 65, 68, 69, 76, 77, 88, 89, 90, 91, 104, 115, 120, 123, 145, 148, 150, 154, 157, 172

Grade 7 2, 5, 8, 11, 13, 14, 16, 18, 21, 23, 25, 27, 30, 31, 34, 35, 40, 41, 46, 47, 52, 53, 54, 55, 58, 59, 64, 65, 68, 69, 72, 73, 76, 77, 80, 81, 88, 89, 90, 91, 93, 94, 104, 107, 110, 113, 115, 116, 118, 120, 123, 125, 127, 129, 131, 133, 136, 139, 142, 143, 145, 148, 150, 152, 154, 156, 158, 167, 168, 173, 174

Grade 8 2, 5, 8, 11, 13, 14, 16, 18, 21, 23, 26, 27, 30, 31, 34, 35, 40, 41, 46, 47, 52, 53, 54, 55, 58, 59, 64, 65, 68, 69, 72, 73, 78, 79, 80, 81, 88, 89, 90, 91, 93, 94, 97, 99, 100, 104, 107, 110, 113, 115, 116, 118, 120, 123, 125, 128, 129, 131, 133, 136, 139, 142, 143, 145, 148, 150, 152, 155, 156, 157, 158, 159, 160, 166, 167, 168, 173, 174, 175

Recommended speeds

The following recommended *minimum* speeds are given as a general guide. It is essential that scales and arpeggios are played at a speed rapid enough to allow well-organized breathing, yet steady enough to allow a well-focused sound with good intonation across the range.

Trombone

major and minor scales, chromatic scales, whole-tone scales, dominant and diminished sevenths

major and minor arpeggios

Grade 1	♩	=	44		♪	=	66
Grade 2	♩	=	48		♪	=	72
Grade 3	♩	=	56		♪	=	84
Grade 4	♩	=	63		♪	=	92
Grade 5	♩	=	72		♪	=	104
Grade 6	♩	=	96		♩.	=	46
Grade 7	♩	=	108		♩.	=	56
Grade 8	♩	=	120		♩.	=	60

Valved instruments

major and minor scales, chromatic scales, whole-tone scales, dominant and diminished sevenths

major and minor arpeggios

Grade 1	♩	=	50		♪	=	72
Grade 2	♩	=	56		♪	=	80
Grade 3	♩	=	66		♪	=	92
Grade 4	♩	=	72		♪	=	100
Grade 5	♩	=	80		♪	=	112
Grade 6	♩	=	104		♩.	=	56
Grade 7	♩	=	116		♩.	=	66
Grade 8	♩	=	132		♩.	=	76

Major Scales

1 C MAJOR 1 Octave

1 **All instruments**: keep the tone as full as possible as you ascend.
Valved instruments: listen carefully to the intonation of both Cs,
compensating with the 4th valve where available.
Trombone: tune E carefully.

2 C MAJOR A Twelfth

2 **Valved instruments**: take care to keep the highest notes of this scale (especially G³) really centred.

3 C MAJOR 2 Octaves

3 **Bass Trombone**: co-ordinate the slide and 'F' valve carefully.

4 D♭ MAJOR 1 Octave

4 **Valved instruments**: fingering 2+3 to 1 and back (D♭ to F) needs
careful co-ordination.
Trombone: tune low D♭ and G♭ carefully.

5 D♭ MAJOR A Twelfth

6 D♭ MAJOR 2 Octaves

7 D MAJOR 1 Octave

7 **Valved instruments**: co-ordinate the fingering from F♯ to G
carefully (2+3 to 1+2).

8 D MAJOR A Twelfth

9 D MAJOR 2 Octaves

10 Eb MAJOR 1 Octave

10 Valved instruments: listen carefully to top Eb which tends to be
sharp. Use 1+4 for top Eb if the 4th valve is available.
Trombone: do not let the tone thin out as you ascend.

11 Eb MAJOR A Twelfth

11 Valved instruments: listen carefully to the intonation of top Bb, which may be flat. Do not just press
harder on the mouthpiece for the highest notes; keep the corners of the embouchure still.
Trombone: remember to maintain a firm diaphragm support throughout, especially at the top over the
turn-around. Do not relax the embouchure too soon.

12 Eb MAJOR 2 Octaves

13 E MAJOR 2 Octaves

13 All instruments: take care with the production of the lowest notes in this scale; keep the tone as uniform
as possible.
Euphonium: use 2+4 for E¹ if the 4th valve is available.

14 F MAJOR 2 Octaves

14 Valved instruments: special care must be taken to preserve uniformity of tone and intonation across the
range.
Euphonium: use the 4th valve where available for F¹.

15 F# MAJOR A Twelfth

15 Valved instruments: low B needs careful tuning; compensate with the 4th valve where available.

16 F# MAJOR 2 Octaves

16 Valved instruments: special care must be taken to preserve uniformity of tone and intonation across the
range. Low B needs careful tuning; compensate with the 4th valve where available.
Trombone: top F# (F#³) tends to be flat; tune it carefully.

17 G MAJOR A Twelfth

17 Valved instruments: listen carefully to the intonation of low B and C, compensating with the 4th valve where available.
Trombone: make sure that you extend the slide fully to 7th position for low B; use the 'F' valve alternative (V²) where available.

18 G MAJOR 2 Octaves

18 Valved instruments: take care to centre both pitch and tone of the top three notes of this scale.
Trombone: top G tends to be flat; tune it carefully.

19 A♭ MAJOR 1 Octave

19 Valved instruments: listen carefully to the intonation on low C, compensating with the 4th valve where available.
Trombone: listen carefully to the tuning of D♭, both ascending and descending.

20 A♭ MAJOR A Twelfth

20 Valved instruments: listen carefully to top E♭, which tends to be sharp. Use 1+4 for top E♭ if the 4th valve is available.

21 A♭ MAJOR 2 Octaves

21 Valved instruments: listen carefully to top E♭ and F, which tend to be sharp. Use 1+4 and 4 respectively for these notes, where the 4th valve is available.
Trombone: top A♭ will need extra diaphragm support to maintain the tonal uniformity of this scale.

22 A MAJOR A Twelfth

22 and 23 Trombone: make sure that you extend the slide fully to 7th position for low B, tuning the following C♯ really carefully. Where available, use the 'F' valve alternative (V²), listening carefully to the intonation.

23 A MAJOR 2 Octaves

23 Valved instruments: listen carefully to top A which tends to be flat.

24 B♭ MAJOR 1 Octave

24 Valved instruments: make sure that 3 goes down simultaneously with 1 on C. Listen carefully to the intonation on C, using the 4th valve (where available) to compensate. Do not let the tone thin out as you ascend.

Trombone: in order to avoid sharpness, make sure that you extend the slide fully to 6th position for C.

25 B♭ MAJOR A Twelfth

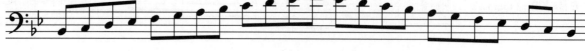

26 B♭ MAJOR 2 Octaves

27 B MAJOR A Twelfth

27 Trombone: calculate the slide positions carefully at the top of this scale in order to avoid intonation problems.

Minor Scales

28 C MINOR melodic 1 Octave

28 and 29 All instruments: keep the tone as full as possible as you ascend.

Valved instruments: listen carefully to the intonation of both Cs, compensating with the 4th valve where available.

29 C MINOR harmonic 1 Octave

30 C MINOR melodic A Twelfth

30 and 31 Trombone: top G tends to be flat; tune it carefully.

31 C MINOR harmonic A Twelfth

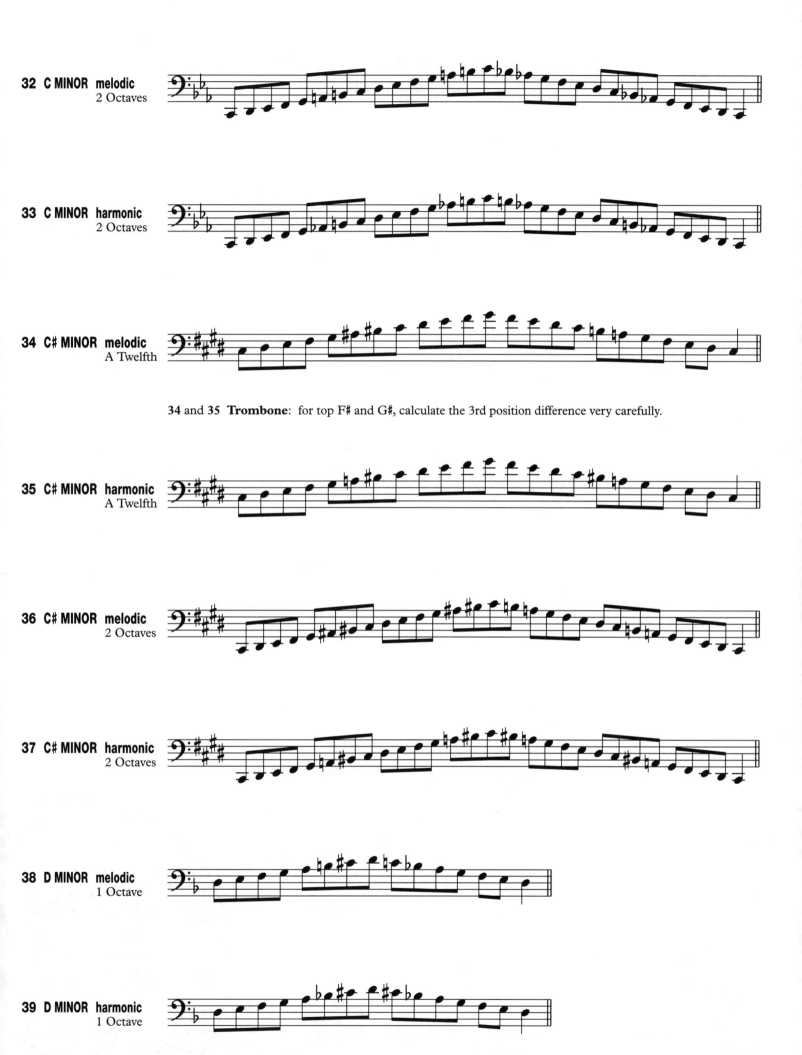

34 and **35** **Trombone**: for top F♯ and G♯, calculate the 3rd position difference very carefully.

39 **Trombone**: the interval B♭ to C♯ needs careful pitching.

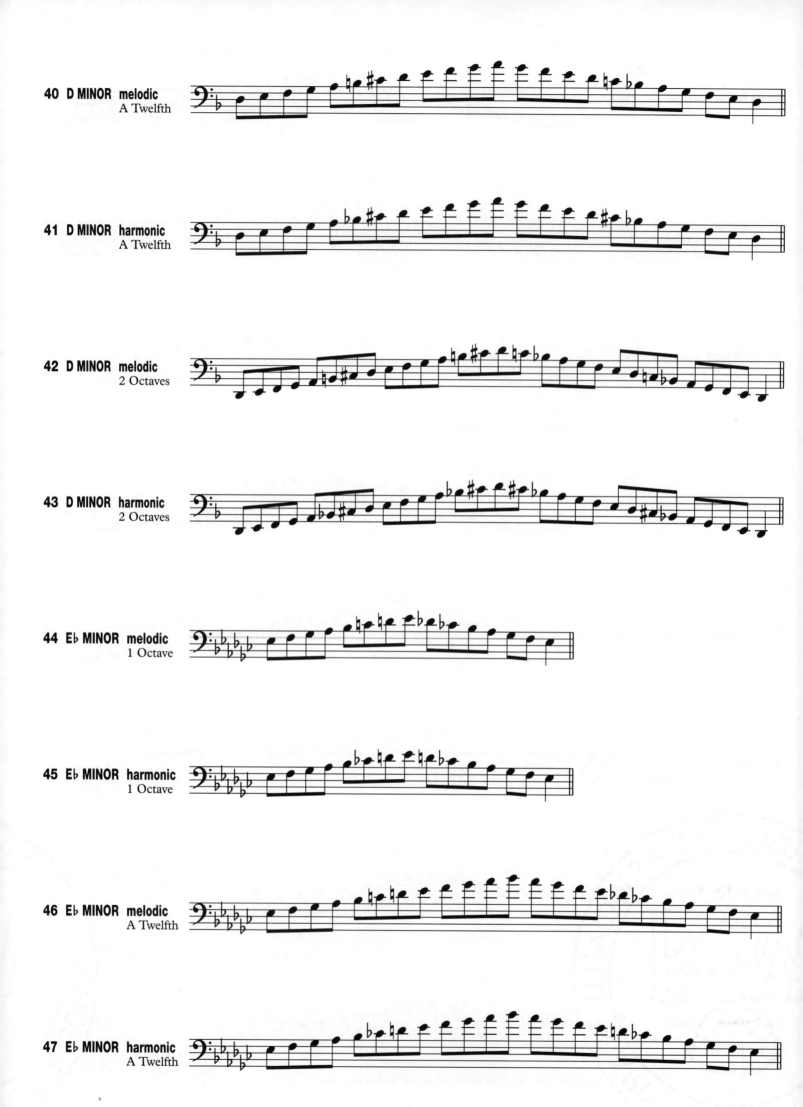

48 E♭ MINOR melodic 2 Octaves

49 E♭ MINOR harmonic 2 Octaves

50 E MINOR melodic 1 Octave

50 and 51 **Trombone**: listen carefully to the intonation of top D♯.

51 E MINOR harmonic 1 Octave

52 E MINOR melodic 2 Octaves

53 E MINOR harmonic 2 Octaves

54 F MINOR melodic 2 Octaves

54 and 55 **Valved instruments**: special care must be taken to preserve uniformity of tone and intonation across the range. Top E♭, E and F will tend to be sharp; use 1+4, 2+4 and 4 for these notes where the 4th valve is available.

Euphonium: use the 4th valve where available for F¹.

55 F MINOR harmonic 2 Octaves

56 F♯ MINOR melodic
A Twelfth

57 F♯ MINOR harmonic
A Twelfth

58 F♯ MINOR melodic
2 Octaves

59 F♯ MINOR harmonic
2 Octaves

60 G MINOR melodic
1 Octave

60 and **61 All instruments**: take care with the production of the lowest notes of these scales. Keep the tone as uniform and as focused as possible.

61 G MINOR harmonic
1 Octave

61 Valved instruments: fingering 1 to 2+3 and back (E♭ to F♯) needs careful co-ordination.

62 G MINOR melodic
A Twelfth

63 G MINOR harmonic
A Twelfth

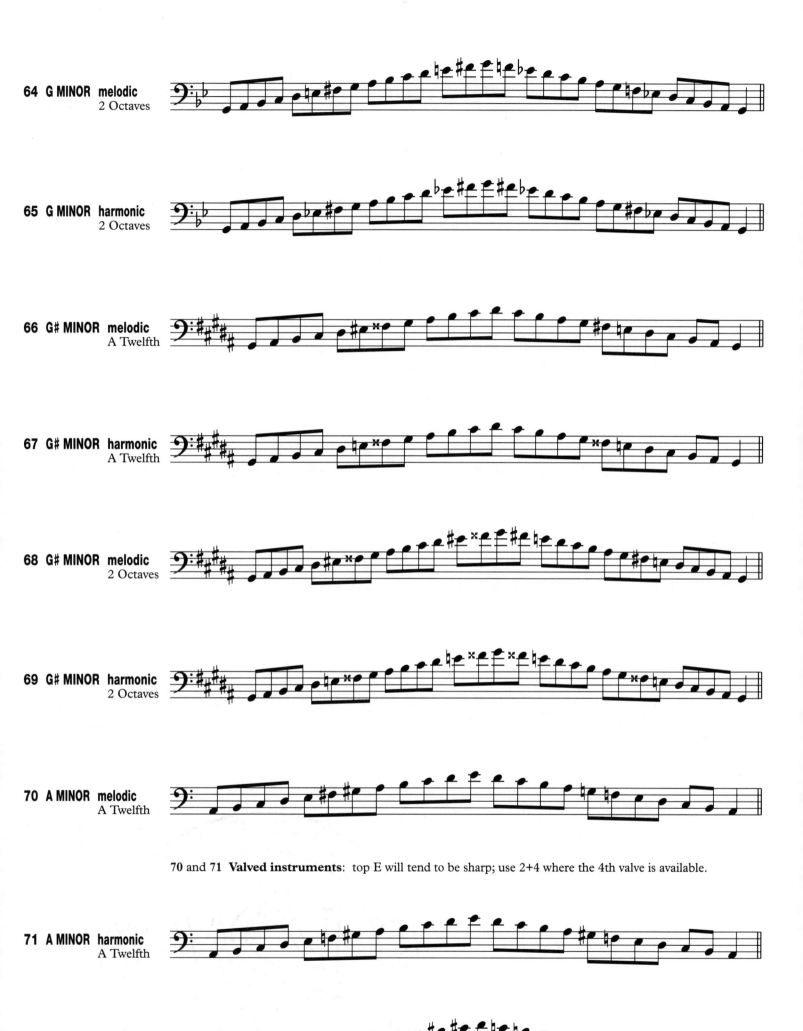

64 G MINOR melodic
2 Octaves

65 G MINOR harmonic
2 Octaves

66 G# MINOR melodic
A Twelfth

67 G# MINOR harmonic
A Twelfth

68 G# MINOR melodic
2 Octaves

69 G# MINOR harmonic
2 Octaves

70 A MINOR melodic
A Twelfth

70 and **71 Valved instruments**: top E will tend to be sharp; use 2+4 where the 4th valve is available.

71 A MINOR harmonic
A Twelfth

72 A MINOR melodic
2 Octaves

73 A MINOR harmonic
2 Octaves

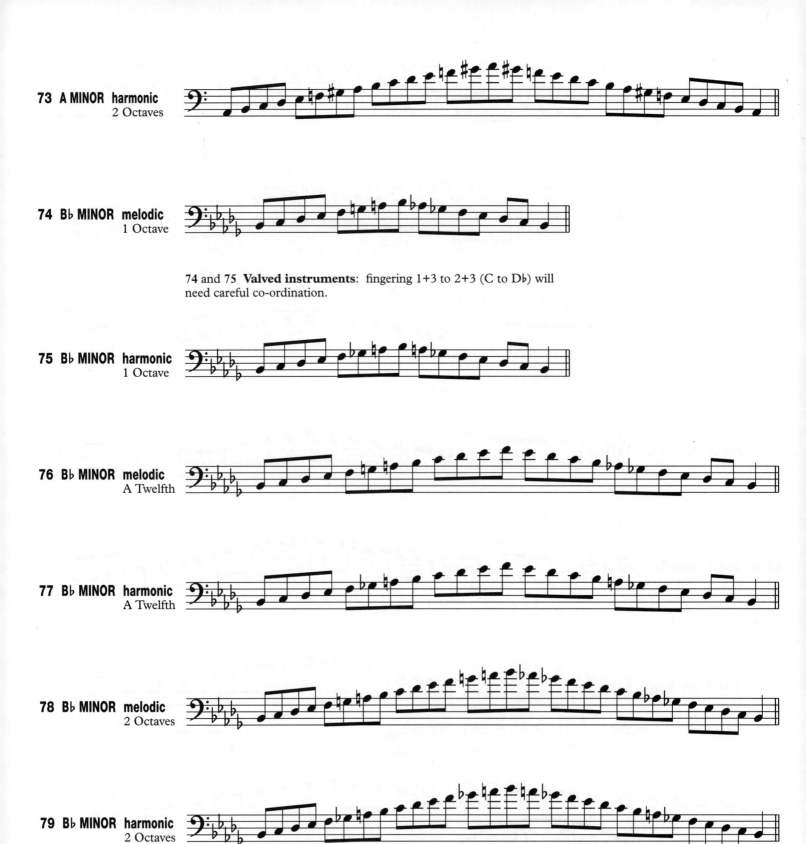

74 B♭ MINOR melodic
1 Octave

74 and 75 **Valved instruments**: fingering 1+3 to 2+3 (C to D♭) will need careful co-ordination.

75 B♭ MINOR harmonic
1 Octave

76 B♭ MINOR melodic
A Twelfth

77 B♭ MINOR harmonic
A Twelfth

78 B♭ MINOR melodic
2 Octaves

79 B♭ MINOR harmonic
2 Octaves

80 B MINOR melodic
A Twelfth

81 B MINOR harmonic
A Twelfth

Chromatic Scales

NOTE: the breath must be gauged very carefully for 2-octave chromatic scales.

Euphonium: where available, the use of the 4th valve is essential in the chromatic scale, both to aid intonation and develop fluency in its use.

Trombone: in all chromatic scales, take special care to keep the slide movement quick and precise.

82 on C 1 Octave

82 Trombone: the slide movement between F and F♯ needs careful negotiation.

83 on C 2 Octaves

84 on C♯ 2 Octaves

85 on D 2 Octaves

86 on E♭ 1 Octave

87 on E♭ 2 Octaves

88 on E 2 Octaves

88-91 All instruments: aim to preserve uniformity of sound throughout the range, especially when descending.

89 on F 2 Octaves

89 Trombone: if using the 'F' valve, co-ordinate slide and LH thumb movement carefully.

90 on F# 2 Octaves

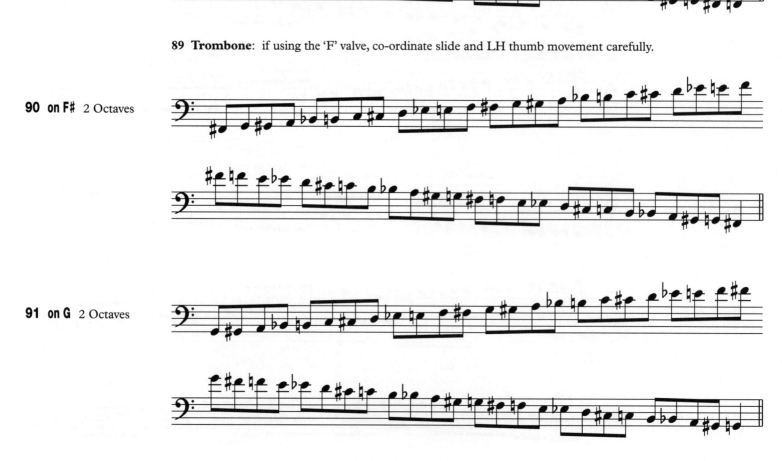

91 on G 2 Octaves

92 on A♭ A Twelfth

92 Valved instruments: top E♭ will tend to be sharp; use 1+4 for this note where the 4th valve is available.

93 on A♭ 2 Octaves

93 Trombone: top A♭ will need extra support to maintain the tonal uniformity of this scale.

94 on A 2 Octaves

95 on B♭ 1 Octave

95 Valved instruments: listen carefully to the intonation of low B and C, compensating with the 4th valve where available.

96 on B♭ A Twelfth

97 on B♭ 2 Octaves

98 on B 2 Octaves

98 Bass Trombone: as the 'F' valve slide needs to be extended to obtain low B (B¹), the ordinary slide will need careful positioning to ensure secure intonation throughout.

Whole-Tone Scales

99 on A 2 Octaves

100 on B♭ 2 Octaves

101 on D 2 Octaves

102 on E♭ 2 Octaves

Major Arpeggios

103 C MAJOR 1 Octave

103 Valved instruments: finger co-ordination needs care throughout, especially when slurred; using the 4th valve on the euphonium will eradicate this problem and improve intonation.

104 C MAJOR A Twelfth

104 All instruments: keep a really centred sound on top G.

105 C MAJOR 2 Octaves

106 Db MAJOR 1 Octave

107 Db MAJOR A Twelfth

108 Db MAJOR 2 Octaves

109 D MAJOR 1 Octave

110 D MAJOR A Twelfth

111 D MAJOR 2 Octaves

112 E♭ MAJOR 1 Octave

112 **Trombone**: support the sound carefully from B♭ to E♭ and back, especially when *legato*-tonguing.

113 E♭ MAJOR A Twelfth

114 E♭ MAJOR 2 Octaves

115 E MAJOR 2 Octaves

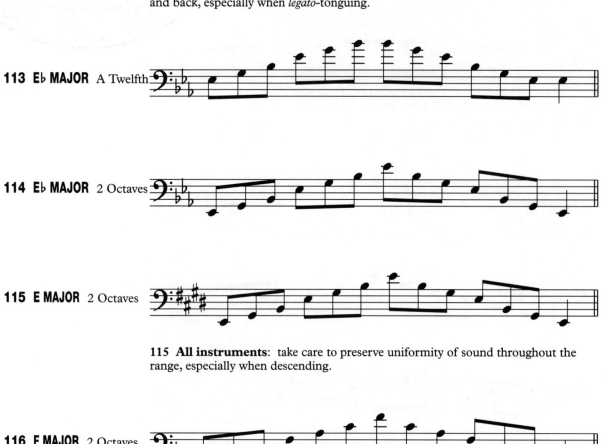

115 **All instruments**: take care to preserve uniformity of sound throughout the range, especially when descending.

116 F MAJOR 2 Octaves

117 F# MAJOR A Twelfth

118 F# MAJOR 2 Octaves

119 G MAJOR A Twelfth

120 G MAJOR 2 Octaves

121 A♭ MAJOR 1 Octave

121 Valved instruments: listen carefully to the intonation on C, compensating with the 4th valve where available.

122 A♭ MAJOR A Twelfth

122 and 123 Valved instruments: as most notes in these arpeggios are played with the 1st valve, lip flexibility must be carefully calculated, especially when slurred.

123 A♭ MAJOR 2 Octaves

124 A MAJOR A Twelfth

125 A MAJOR 2 Octaves

126 B♭ MAJOR 1 Octave

126 All instruments: take special care when negotiating F to B♭ and back, especially when slurred or *legato*-tongued.

127 B♭ MAJOR A Twelfth

128 B♭ MAJOR 2 Octaves

128 Trombone: calculate the interval between top F and top B♭ really carefully (top B♭ often emerges as top A♭).

129 B MAJOR A Twelfth

129 Trombone: for top D♯ and F♯, calculate the 3rd position difference very carefully.

Minor Arpeggios

130 C MINOR 1 Octave

130 Valved instruments: listen carefully to the intonation on low C, compensating with the 4th valve where available.

131 C MINOR A Twelfth

132 C MINOR 2 Octaves

133 C# MINOR A Twelfth

134 C# MINOR 2 Octaves

135 D MINOR 1 Octave

135 Trombone: take special care to support the sound from A to D and back, especially when *legato*-tonguing.

136 D MINOR A Twelfth

137 D MINOR 2 Octaves

138 Eb MINOR 1 Octave

139 E♭ MINOR A Twelfth

140 E♭ MINOR 2 Octaves

141 E MINOR 1 Octave

142 E MINOR 2 Octaves

143 F MINOR 2 Octaves

143 All instruments: take care to preserve uniformity of sound throughout the range, especially when descending.

144 F♯ MINOR A Twelfth

145 F♯ MINOR 2 Octaves

146 G MINOR 1 Octave

146 Valved instruments: keep the tone on low G as steady as possible. Take special care when negotiating D to G and back, especially when slurred.

147 G MINOR A Twelfth

147 and **148 Valved instruments**: lip flexibility needs care here, especially when slurred.

148 G MINOR 2 Octaves

149 G# MINOR A Twelfth

150 G# MINOR 2 Octaves

150 Valved instruments: take care when negotiating top D# to top G# and back, especially when slurred.

151 A MINOR A Twelfth

152 A MINOR 2 Octaves

153 B♭ MINOR 1 Octave

154 B♭ MINOR A Twelfth

155 B♭ MINOR 2 Octaves

155 Trombone: calculate the interval between top F and top B♭ really carefully (top B♭ often emerges as top A♭).

156 B MINOR A Twelfth

156 Valved instruments: listen carefully to the intonation on low B, compensating with the 4th valve where available.

Dominant Sevenths

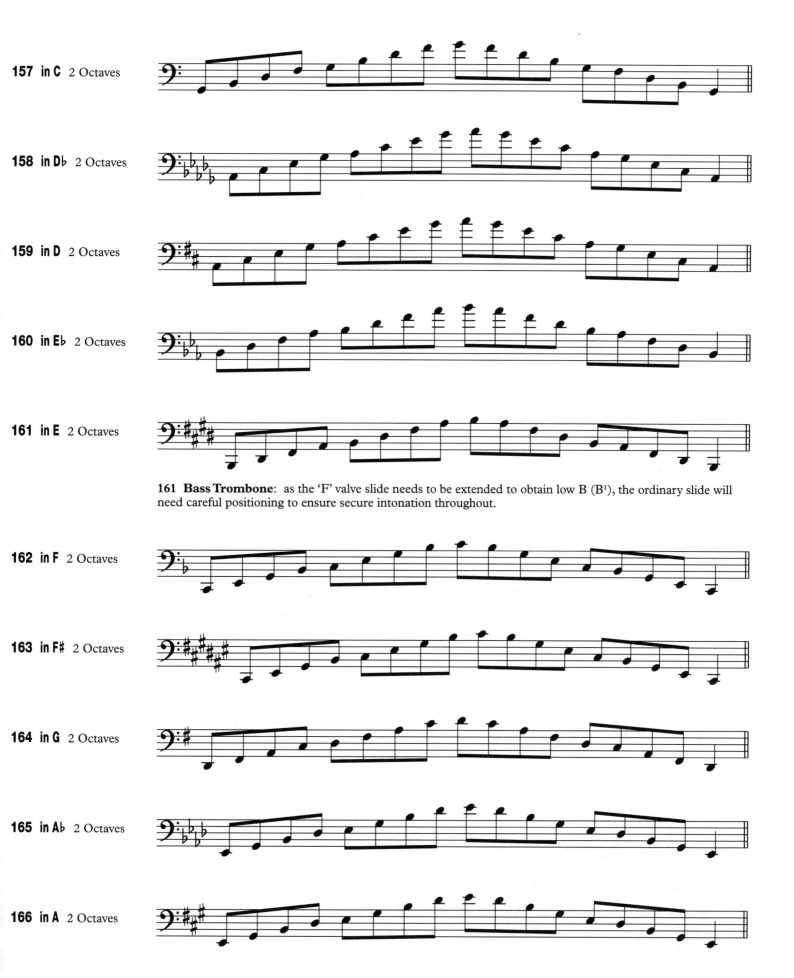

161 Bass Trombone: as the 'F' valve slide needs to be extended to obtain low B (B¹), the ordinary slide will need careful positioning to ensure secure intonation throughout.

Diminished Sevenths

173 Valved instruments: take care with the fingering co-ordination of the lower notes in this arpeggio.

AB 2481

Music and text origination by
Barnes Music Engraving Ltd, East Sussex
Printed by Caligraving Ltd, Thetford, Norfolk

7:03